Grayslake Area Public Library District

Grayslake, Illinois

1. A fine will be charged on each book which is not returned when it is due.

2. All injuries to books beyond reasonable wear and all losses shall be made good to the satisfaction of the Librarian.

3. Each borrower is held responsible for all books drawn on his card and for all fines accruing on the same.

The Great
Thanksgiving Escape

To my family and those get-togethers
that unraveled beautifully.

First edition 2014

Library of Congress Catalog Card Number pending
ISBN 978-0-7636-6306-3

CCP 19 18 17 16 15 14
10 9 8 7 6 5 4 3 2 1

Printed in Shenzhen, Guangdong, China

This book was typeset in Adobe Garamond.
The illustrations were done in pencil and completed digitally.

Candlewick Press
99 Dover Street
Somerville, Massachusetts 02144

visit us at www.candlewick.com

The Great
Thanksgiving Escape

MARK FEARING

CANDLEWICK PRESS

It was another
Thanksgiving
at Grandma's.

"You can play in here with the rest of the kids," Gavin's mother told him. "We'll call you when the turkey's ready."

"Have fun!" Gavin's dad called.
But Gavin knew it was not going to be fun.
Not fun at all.

"Hey," someone whispered. It was his cousin Rhonda. "What do you say we break out of here and head for the swing set in the backyard?"

"I'm supposed to stay here until turkey time," Gavin said.

Rhonda climbed out from under the coats.

"The way I see it, Gav," she said, "is that sometimes you have to make your own fun."

"Are you with me?" she asked.

Gavin nodded. "I'm in."

They crept out and headed for the front door.

Suddenly, Rhonda jumped back.
"That way's blocked by vicious guard dogs.
I think they've picked up our scent!" she yelled.

"Run!"

But when they rounded the corner,
Rhonda stopped dead in her tracks.

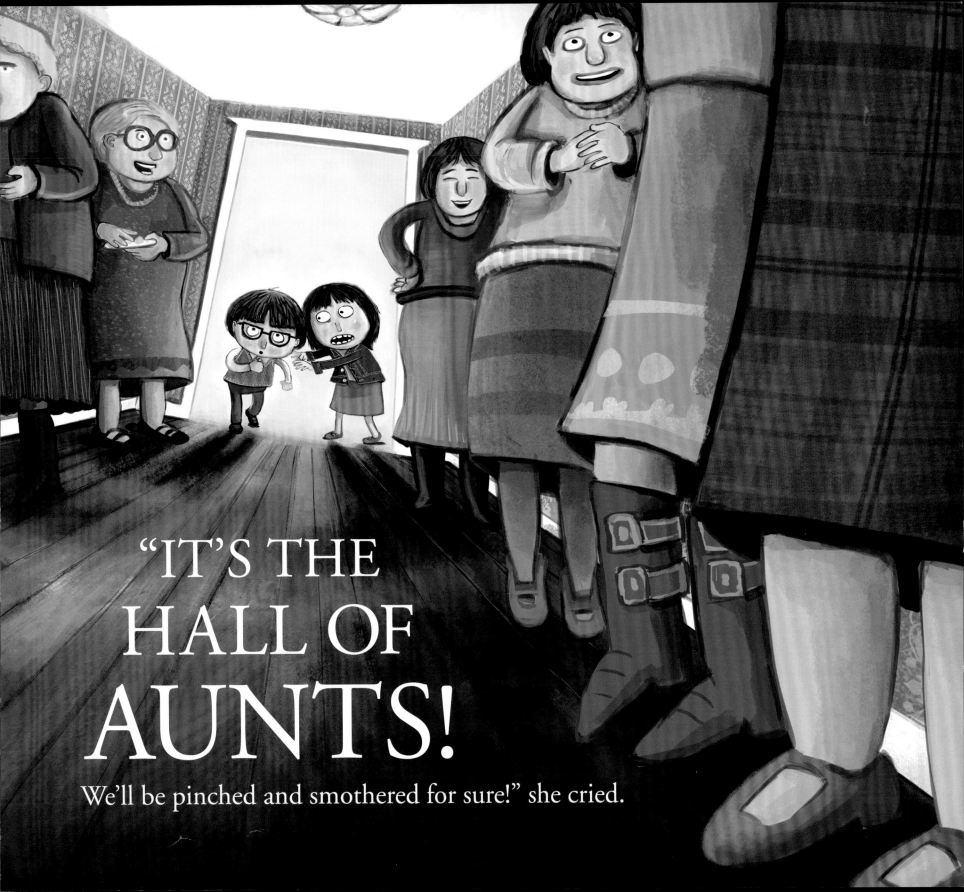

"IT'S THE HALL OF AUNTS!

We'll be pinched and smothered for sure!" she cried.

Gavin trembled, remembering Christmas last year.
He'd had to ice his face for three days.

They took off, but it was too late.
Rhonda had been grabbed.

Luckily she reacted defensively

and managed to break free
without a pinch.

"Quick, before another one comes in for a snuggle!" yelled Rhonda as she bolted past.

"Head for the back door!"

"OH, NO—
THE GREAT
WALL OF
BUTTS!"

Rhonda yelled, "It's certain death to get between them and the TV!"

"Down here," said Rhonda. "I bet there's
a way through the basement."

Gavin wasn't so sure. It looked dark and
smelled like dirty socks and hair gel.

They peeked cautiously around the corner.

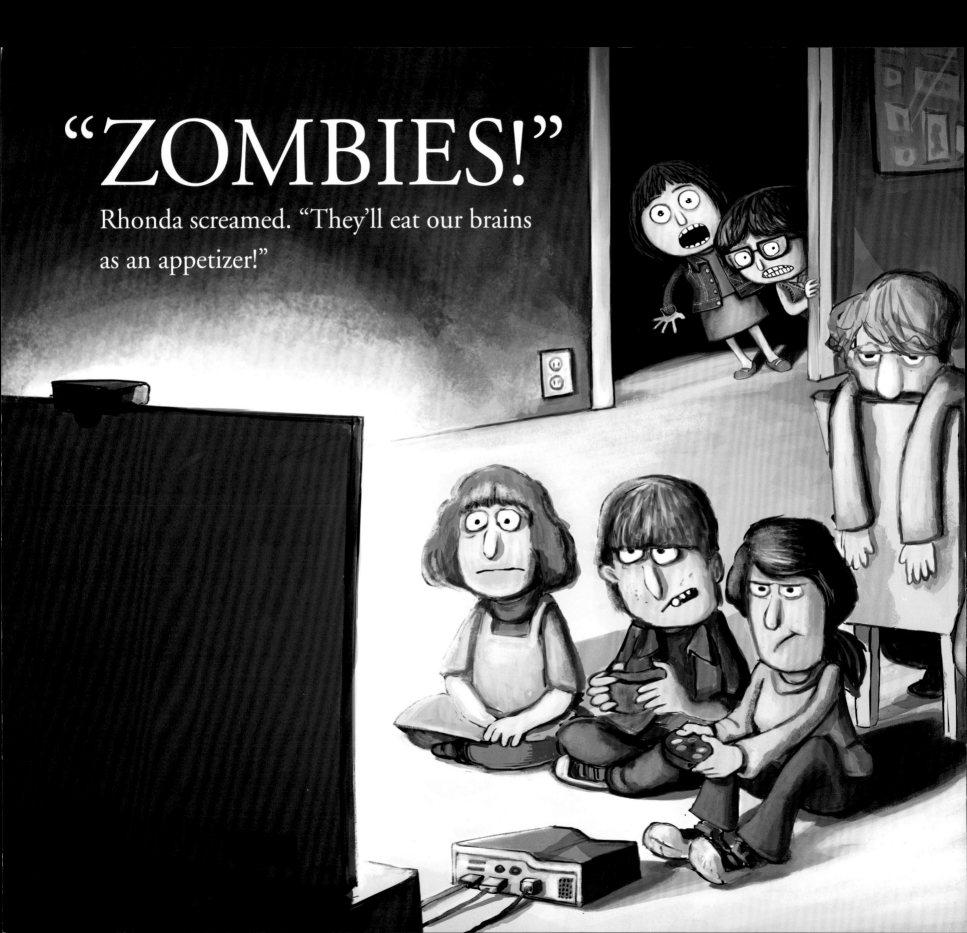

"ZOMBIES!"

Rhonda screamed. "They'll eat our brains as an appetizer!"

They raced back up the stairs to the kitchen.
"Just a little snack for the road," Gavin said.
"No!" Rhonda yelled.

"It's a trap!"

She grabbed Gavin just before they were surrounded.

They turned and sprinted for the door.

"We're almost there!"

But they skidded to a stop
when they reached the glass.

"At least we tried," Rhonda said.
Gavin was quiet for a moment.

Then he said, "The way I see it, Rhonda, is that
sometimes you have to make your own fun."